Bastet

Bastet was a much-loved Egyptian goddess, believed to protect people from disease and evil. Hundreds of thousands of Egyptians attended the annual festivals held in her honor. Sometimes Bastet was portrayed as a cat, sometimes as a woman with a cat's head. When Bastet was portrayed as a woman, she carried a musical instrument called a sistrum in her right hand and a small shield adorned with a lioness's head in her left hand. Usually sh[e]
basket and had figurines of kittens at her fe[et]

Tutankhamun

[beca]me pharaoh in 1332 B.C., when he was only nine [and died] at the age of eighteen. His tomb, which was [discovered in 192]?, was the only Egyptian royal tomb found in [Egypt tha]t had not been plundered by grave robbers. [The to]mb contained over 2000 objects, many of them [made of gold and o]ther precious materials. Most of these items are at [the museu]m in Cairo.

Mummies

Early Egyptians believed that if a person wanted to live on after death, his or her body had to be preserved. The Egyptians developed elaborate methods for doing this, which involved drying the body with salt and wrapping it in linen bandages. A portrait mask was sometimes placed on the mummy. When an Egyptian pharaoh died, his mummy was placed in a mummy coffin and, together with items the pharaoh would need in the afterlife, buried in a special tomb, sometimes in the shape of a pyramid. Because many valuable objects were buried with the pharaohs, their tombs were inevitably broken into by grave robbers.

The Cat in Ancient Egypt

It is believed that cats were first domesticated in Egypt, probably because they were useful for controlling mice. Very early Egyptian paintings depict cats, often seated under chairs. From being a beloved household animal, cats grew to be considered sacred and were worshiped. When they died, they were embalmed and wrapped in linen, then taken to special places to be buried. At the end of the nineteenth century, literally tons of cat mummies were discovered when ancient sites were excavated in Egypt.

Gods and Goddesses

Over the long history of Egypt, its people worshiped many gods and goddesses, who took the form of animals, of humans, and of humans with the heads of animals. The ancient Egyptians also worshiped certain animals in their own right, such as sacred bulls, cats, and crocodiles. Although we know a lot about the names of these gods and goddesses and their myths, we do not know very much about the part they played in the lives of the people who worshiped them.

Bastet

Written by Linda Talley

Illustrated by Itoko Maeno

MarshMedia, Kansas City, Missouri

For Brennan and Sara. — L.T.

For M. — I.M.

Text © 2001 by Marsh Film Enterprises, Inc.

Illustrations © 2001 by Itoko Maeno

Published by **MARSH**media

A Division of Marsh Film Enterprises, Inc.
P. O. Box 8082
Shawnee Mission, KS 66208

Library of Congress Cataloging–in–Publication Data
Talley, Linda.
    Bastet / written by Linda Talley; illustrated by Itoko Maeno.
        p.   cm.
    Summary: Bastet, a golden cat, shares her life on the streets of Cairo, Egypt,
with her best friend Sabah, until a pampered cat tries to lure her away with the
promise of getting into the Egyptian Museum to see Tutankhamun's golden mask.
      ISBN 1–55942–161–4
      [1. Cats—Fiction. 2. Friendship—Fiction. 3. Cairo (Egypt)—Fiction.]
I. Maeno, Itoko, ill. II. Title.
PZ7.T156355Bas 2000
[Fic]—dc21   00-060947

Book layout and typography by Cirrus Design

Special thanks to Minnie, Rosie, Blondie,

and Carrot for technical assistance.

Printed in Hong Kong

Motorbikes and pushcarts. Silversmiths and goldsmiths. Tent-makers and fortune-tellers. Coffee shops and kebab houses. Fragrance of falafel and fresh fruit. Copper pots and carpets, sandals and scarabs, buttons and baskets, jewelry and galabias.

This is the Khan el–Khalili bazaar!
But wait. The picture is incomplete!

On this narrow street of
the Khan el-Khalili sit two cats,
one golden and one spotted. The first
is called Bastet. The other, Sabah. Bastet and
Sabah are very best friends, and the Khan
el-Khalili is their home.

Their lives are not easy, but the cats are happy. They prowl the cafes for the stray bit of kebab. Together.

They explore every corner of the bazaar. Together.

They sleep on a scrap of worn carpet tossed out the back door of a shop. Together.

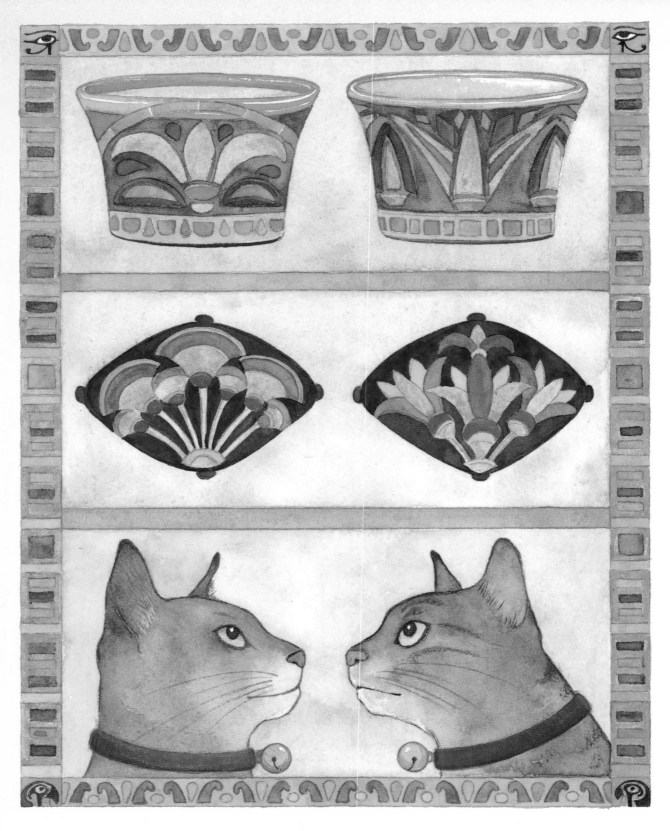

And together they dream of a different life. A real home. Bowls of milk for breakfast. Pillows to sleep on through the hot afternoons. Brightly colored collars with little gold bells. These are, perhaps, the dreams of all cats who make their homes on the street.

But beyond these dreams, beyond the milk and pillows and little gold bells, Bastet and Sabah have always had a special dream that belongs to just the two of them.

Their dream—to see the golden mask of Tutankhamun.

This mask of pure gleaming gold was placed on the mummy of the young pharaoh Tutankhamun when he was buried in the Egyptian desert centuries ago. Now the mask rests here in Cairo, in the Egyptian Museum.

Bastet and Sabah always knew it was unlikely that two homeless cats would ever be allowed inside the museum. But the possibility was a treasure shared by the two of them.

And then one day, Khufu came to the Khan el-Khalili.

Sabah had found a pita under a vendor's cart and had just started to tear it gently apart. Bastet looked up and saw a dark cat watching them.

Bastet had never seen such a cat. His fur glistened. He wore a red collar with a gold bell dangling below his chin. A few drops of milk clung to his whiskers.

His name was Khufu, and the street was not his home. He had a real home over a shop in the Souk al-Attarin, the spice bazaar. Indeed, he carried with him the scent of cinnamon and cloves. To Bastet's mind he was the most elegant cat on earth. She decided then and there to make him her friend.

Sabah offered Khufu a piece of pita.

"Sabah," said Bastet, "Khufu has already had a breakfast of sweet milk. He doesn't want your dirty scrap of bread!" Bastet knocked the pita into the street with her paw. Sabah looked at Bastet in wide-eyed amazement. Then Sabah turned away. Dodging taxis and motorbikes, she scurried down the street and was gone.

"I guess your friend is a little touchy," said Khufu.

Bastet had never thought of her friend as anything but the most pleasant cat in Cairo, but now she found herself nodding in agreement.

"She's impossible," she said, twitching her tail.

And so, Bastet and Khufu roamed the spice bazaar that day.

He showed her his home and the sunny window where he slept on a brightly embroidered pillow.

In the afternoon, Khufu's master fed them both a meal of choice table scraps in two pretty bowls.

Late in the evening, Bastet found Sabah curled up and asleep on their carpet. Bastet wondered what Sabah had eaten that day.

The next morning, when Sabah awoke, Bastet was carefully grooming herself. Sabah reminded Bastet that they had planned an outing to the fish shop.

"Oh, we can do that some other day," said Bastet. "Khufu has plans for us today!"

Sabah's tail drooped as they made their way toward the spice bazaar. Suddenly Bastet stopped and turned to Sabah with a disapproving look.

"Really, Sabah,"
said Bastet, "You
can't visit Khufu with
those paws!"

Sabah looked at her
paws sadly.

"But Bastet," she said. "They
are my same old paws. A cat who
lives on these streets can't always have
clean paws."

"Well," said Bastet, holding one of her own
paws out for Sabah to inspect, "if you didn't sleep so
late, you would have time to clean them properly, as I
did my own this morning!"

So, in the end, Sabah turned back, and Bastet went on
to the spice bazaar by herself.

That day, Bastet and Khufu walked all the way across Cairo to watch the feluccas sailing down the Nile. As they rested on the quay, Khufu turned to Bastet and said, "You know, you look just like the cats at the museum."

Cats at the museum? No cat would ever be allowed inside the museum! How could Khufu say such a thing?

But Khufu explained everything. There were many cats in the museum—cats in paintings, cats made of bronze and gold. Khufu had seen them. He knew a way in!

Khufu's father had learned the way from an ancient cat who had made his home on the museum grounds. Khufu's father had passed the secret down to Khufu.

And when Bastet told Khufu the dream that she and Sabah had shared for so many years, to see the mask of Tutankhamun, he announced that he would be happy to lead the way into the museum! They would go the very next morning, early, before the museum opened.

Bastet pictured the expression on Sabah's face when she heard that their dream was to come true.

"And Sabah may come too?" Bastet asked Khufu eagerly.

"I think not," said Khufu solemnly. "Two is better."

It was as though a dark cloud had passed before the sun. Khufu saw the troubled look on Bastet's face.

"Just think!" he said. "You will be able to tell Sabah exactly what the mask looks like."

And so, very early the next morning, while Sabah slept soundly on their bit of carpet, Bastet crept away.

"I'll tell you all about it!" she whispered to her sleeping friend.

As Bastet and Khufu ran through the still dark streets of Cairo, Bastet's thoughts kept going back to Sabah.

"Hurry!" called Khufu impatiently. Bastet ran faster.

Finally, the doors of the Egyptian Museum towered over Bastet.

Khufu led her to the grillwork covering a low window. The openings were just large enough for a cat to squeeze through. Into darkness. But Khufu knew the way. He led her over and around piles of boxes, along narrow beams, through dusty passageways.

Bastet followed him as he jumped down into a dimly-lit hall, then as he ran through several rooms and up a wide stairway.

"Hurry!" Khufu called over his shoulder.

Bastet ran as fast as she could—past chests and shrines, couches carved with fantastic animals, thrones and statues—all glittering gold. The treasures from Tutankhamun's tomb!

Bastet turned her head right, then left, then right again. It was impossible! She could never remember it all for Sabah!

She saw Khufu disappear through a doorway.

But Bastet did not follow. She stopped outside the door. She sat. She thought. She remembered everything she and Sabah had heard about Tutankhamun's mask.

The dazzling gold! The ebony eyes! The jeweled cobra! The brilliant inlays of lapis-lazuli and quartz and obsidian!

And in her mind's eye she saw, staring up at Tutankhamun, two scrawny cats, one golden and one spotted. That was her dream, after all. Not just to see the mask, but to see it with Sabah. Together.

How disloyal she had been to Sabah! Now here she was at the museum, chasing after this well-fed cat who kept hissing at her to hurry, hurry, hurry!

But Bastet did not hurry. She did not move at all. She had decided. She would not go in, not without her friend Sabah.

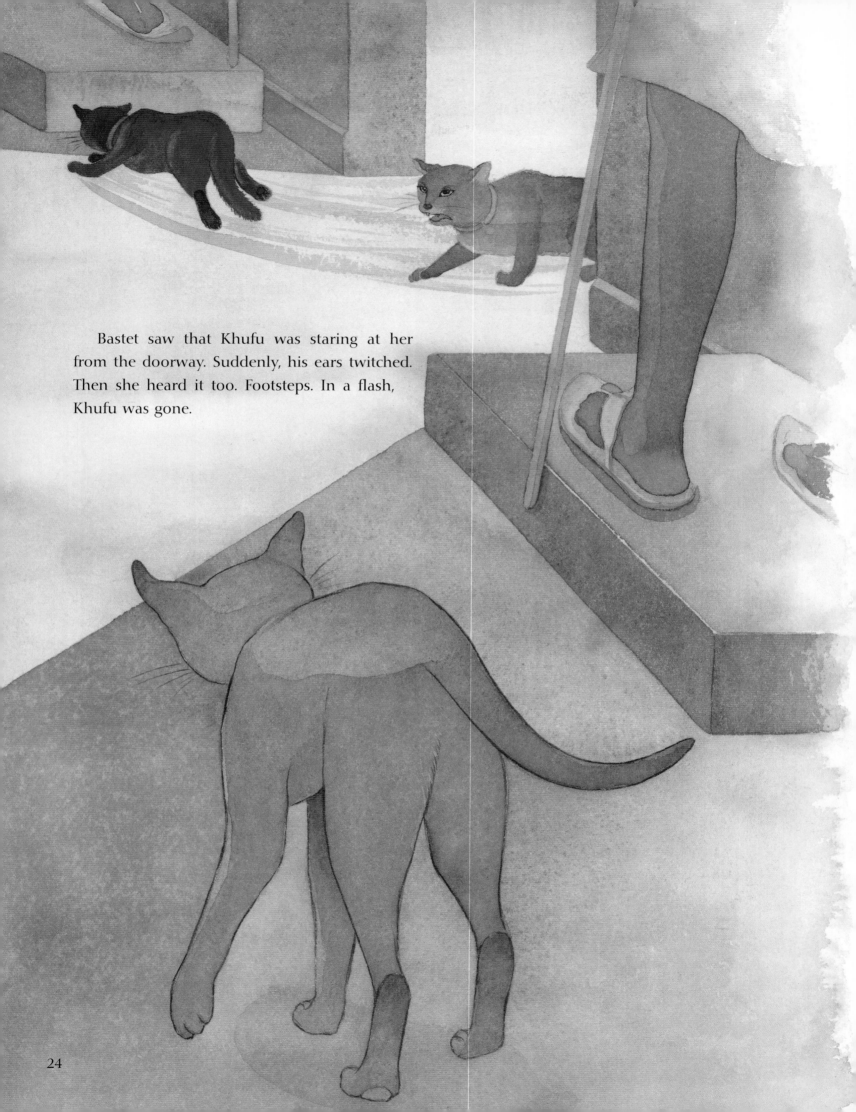

Bastet saw that Khufu was staring at her from the doorway. Suddenly, his ears twitched. Then she heard it too. Footsteps. In a flash, Khufu was gone.

Bastet ran too.

But Bastet had no idea how to get out of the museum.

She ran one direction and then another.

Finally she found a stairway. She was halfway down when the lights went on.

In her fright she rolled down the steps and landed at the feet of a museum guard.

He grabbed her by the back of the neck, took her to the grand doors
of the museum, and tossed her out.

The tall door slammed shut. Bastet's visit to the museum was over.

Bastet made her way home alone that morning. She never saw Khufu again.

After that, Bastet and Sabah were friends as they had always been, but now Bastet knew that she would never trade the treasure of their friendship for anything—not for golden bells, nor pretty pillows—not even for a trip to the museum.

As for that other treasure—Tutankhamun's mask—Bastet never told Sabah that she had very nearly seen it. But sometimes, when she and Sabah lay in the shade talking about their shared dream, Bastet's imaginings seemed more real than they had ever been before.

"Oh, do you think that's what it's really like?" Sabah would ask.

Bastet's answer was always the same.

"Oh, I'm sure it is, my friend! I'm sure it is!"

Dear Parents and Educators,

Friendship is one of life's great gifts. It magnifies our joys and eases our disappointments. Friendship sustains us emotionally, and research has documented that friendship nurtures our physical health as well. People who have a circle of supportive friends enjoy longer and healthier lives.

Learning about friendship can be a challenging and sometimes frustrating experience for children. They may think that our friendships just happen, that they fall into our laps ready-made. Children need to learn that strong personal relationships take time and effort and lots of practice! Many different social skills are needed to form and maintain friendships, and those who have learned problem solving, conflict resolution, and listening skills will be better able to respond when the inevitable disagreements occur.

Friendship embodies the best in human nature: empathy, compassion, self-sacrifice, trust, and—as Bastet discovers—trust's counterpart, loyalty. Encourage children to share their ideas and feelings about Bastet's experiences. Here are some questions to help initiate discussion about the message of *Bastet*.

- How do Bastet and Sabah show that they are friends?

- What is the dream they share?

- In what ways did Bastet behave unkindly to Sabah?

- Why didn't Bastet go into the room to see the mask at the museum?

- What does it mean to be loyal to a friend?

- Describe the friendship between Bastet and Sabah at the end of the story.

- What did you learn from this story about how to treat a friend?

Work to create an environment in your home or classroom where children learn about the pleasures and responsibilities of friendship.

- Celebrate uniqueness in individuals.

- Model and teach active listening skills.

- Teach and practice techniques for conflict resolution.

- Discuss loyalty and what it means to a friendship.

- Celebrate cooperative efforts.

- Praise children for compassionate responses.

- Practice sincere apologies.

- Practice forgiveness

Available from MarshMedia

These storybooks, each hardcover with dust jacket and full-color illustrations throughout, are available at bookstores, or you may order by calling MarshMedia toll free at 1–800–821–3303.

Amazing Mallika, written by Jami Parkison, illustrated by Itoko Maeno. 32 pages. ISBN 1–55942–087–1.

Bailey's Birthday, written by Elizabeth Happy, illustrated by Andra Chase. 32 pages. ISBN 1–55942–059–6.

Bastet, written by Linda Talley, illustrated by Itoko Maeno. 32 pages. ISBN 1–55942–161–4.

Bea's Own Good, written by Linda Talley, illustrated by Andra Chase. 32 pages. ISBN 1–55942–092–8.

Clarissa, written by Carol Talley, illustrated by Itoko Maeno. 32 pages. ISBN 1–55942–014–6.

Emily Breaks Free, written by Linda Talley, illustrated by Andra Chase. 32 pages. ISBN 1–55942–155–X.

Feathers at Las Flores, written by Linda Talley, illustrated by Andra Chase. 32 pages. ISBN 1–55942–162–2.

Following Isabella, written by Linda Talley, illustrated by Andra Chase. 32 pages. ISBN 1–55942–163–0.

Gumbo Goes Downtown, written by Carol Talley, illustrated by Itoko Maeno. 32 pages. ISBN 1–55942–042–1.

Hana's Year, written by Carol Talley, illustrated by Itoko Maeno. 32 pages. ISBN 1–55942–034–0.

Inger's Promise, written by Jami Parkison, illustrated by Andra Chase. 32 pages. ISBN 1–55942–080–4.

Jackson's Plan, written by Linda Talley, illustrated by Andra Chase. 32 pages. ISBN 1–55942–104–5.

Jomo and Mata, written by Alyssa Chase, illustrated by Andra Chase. 32 pages. ISBN 1–55942–051–0.

Kiki and the Cuckoo, written by Elizabeth Happy, illustrated by Andra Chase. 32 pages. ISBN 1–55942–038–3.

Kylie's Concert, written by Patty Sheehan, illustrated by Itoko Maeno. 32 pages. ISBN 1–55942–046–4.

Kylie's Song, written by Patty Sheehan, illustrated by Itoko Maeno. 32 pages. (Advocacy Press) ISBN 0–911655–19–0.

Minou, written by Mindy Bingham, illustrated by Itoko Maeno. 64 pages. (Advocacy Press) ISBN 0–911655–36–0.

Molly's Magic, written by Penelope Colville Paine, illustrated by Itoko Maeno. 32 pages. ISBN 1–55942–068–5.

My Way Sally, written by Mindy Bingham and Penelope Paine, illustrated by Itoko Maeno. 48 pages. (Advocacy Press) ISBN 0–911655–27–1.

Papa Piccolo, written by Carol Talley, illustrated by Itoko Maeno. 32 pages. ISBN 1–55942–028–6.

Pequeña the Burro, written by Jami Parkison, illustrated by Itoko Maeno. 32 pages. ISBN 1–55942–055–3.

Plato's Journey, written by Linda Talley, illustrated by Itoko Maeno. 32 pages. ISBN 1–55942–100–2.

Tessa on Her Own, written by Alyssa Chase, illustrated by Itoko Maeno. 32 pages. ISBN 1–55942–064–2.

Thank You, Meiling, written by Linda Talley, illustrated by Itoko Maeno. 32 pages. ISBN 1–55942–118–5.

Time for Horatio, written by Penelope Paine, illustrated by Itoko Maeno. 48 pages. (Advocacy Press) ISBN 0–911655–33–6.

Toad in Town, written by Linda Talley, illustrated by Itoko Maeno. 32 pages. ISBN 1–55942–165–7.

Tonia the Tree, written by Sandy Stryker, illustrated by Itoko Maeno. 32 pages. (Advocacy Press) ISBN 0–911655–16–6.

Companion videos and activity guides, as well as multimedia kits for classroom use, are also available. MarshMedia has been publishing high-quality, award–winning learning materials for children since 1969. To order or to receive a free catalog, call 1–800–821–3303, or visit us at www.marshmedia.com.

Cairo

Cairo, the capital of Egypt and the largest city in Africa, sits on the Nile River in Northern Egypt. At the city's heart are modern skyscrapers, office buildings, high–rise hotels and apartment buildings, as well as cinemas and department stores. Surrounding this area are the old quarters of the city, where ancient buildings line twisting streets, too narrow in some cases for automobile use.

Galabia

While many Egyptians wear Western–style clothing, the traditional *galabia* is common attire in both rural and urban areas. A *galabia* is a long, loose, shirt–like garment with long, full sleeves. It is an ideal garment for the Egyptian climate because its construction allows both cooling ventilation and ample protection from the sun. Many travelers to Egypt take a *galabia* home as a souvenir of their visit.

Mosques

Islam is the religion preached by the prophet Muhammad, who was born in Mecca, Saudi Arabia, in about 570 A.D. Followers of this religion are called Muslims. Islam is the official religion of Egypt. A mosque is the Muslim place of worship. Faithful Muslims must pray five times a day—at sunrise, noon, afternoon, sunset and at night. Most mosques have one or more minarets, or towers, from which a crier chants the call to prayer at the appointed times. There are hundreds of mosques in the city of Cairo, many dating from medieval times. It is said that no matter where one is standing in Cairo, one is able to see a minaret.

Felucca

Anyone standing by the Nile a thousand years ago would have seen small narrow boats called *feluccas* sailing by. The same boats still sail the Nile. A cruise on a *felucca* may last five days or an hour, but it is an adventure few visitors to Egypt pass up.

Bazaars

A bazaar is a marketplace or street of many small shops and stalls. The old quarter of Islamic Cairo, sometimes called the Old Town, has many bazaars. None is more famous than the Khan el–Khalili, which began in 1382 as a stopover for caravans and became one of the largest bazaars in the Middle East.